Nina and MADISON

Ride the Bus in Seattle

This book is published by Lifevest Publishing Inc., Centennial, Colorado. No portion of this book may be reproduced without the expressed written consent of Lifevest Publishing or Tara Jorgensen.

Nina and Madison Ride the Bus in Seattle
is written and illustrated by Tara Jorgensen
Copyright 2007 © Tara Jorgensen

Published and Printed by:
Lifevest Publishing
4901 E. Dry Creek Rd., #170
Centennial, CO 80122
www.lifevestpublishing.com

Printed in the United States of America

I.S.B.N. 1-59879-329-2

Nina and MADISON

Ride the Bus in Seattle

Written and Illustrated
by Tara Jorgensen

"Hi Madison, do you want to ride to the city on the bus today?" questions Nina on the other end of the phone.

"Sounds like fun," says Madison. "I'll meet you at the bus stop."

"There are too many choices." Nina sighs as she looks at the Lake Forest Park bus schedule.   "Let's hop on the next bus and see where it takes us."

"Madison, I see a bus coming. Let's get on," Nina says.

Nina climbs the steps and goes to the back of the bus.

Madison notices his shoe lace is loose. He moves aside, and it takes him a moment to tie it. When he finishes, he hops on the bus.

Nina waits patiently for Madison. She waits and waits. Nina wonders if Madison decided to stay home.

"Oh No!" exclaims Madison. He realizes he is on the wrong bus. "This bus is already moving, and it's too late to switch!"

Madison's bus brings him all the way to Fremont. It has been a long, bumpy ride, so he decides to get off and walk around.

He doesn't see Nina. Instead, he sees a giant troll statue under a bridge. The troll looks a little unusual, but Madison decides to be brave. "This must have taken the artist a LONG time to make. Good thing it isn't real," Madison whispers to himself.

Nina's bus isn't going to Fremont. It's streaming towards downtown. She looks out her bus window and sees the Space Needle. She wonders where Madison is and hopes he is safe.

The bus Nina is on finally stops at the Pike Place Market. There sits a fruit stand selling delicious apples and juicy pears.

Rumble, rumble goes her tummy. She buys an apple for sixty-nine cents. It is crisp and juicy.

Madison explores Fremont. There is so much to do and see--bright colors, curvy buildings, and statues wearing real clothes.

After walking a long time, he ends up far from Fremont at The Ballard Locks. Madison eats and watches the fish jump.

"Wowee, owee, my feet are sore," moans Madison, "I need to find another bus."

Nina decides it is time to leave Pike Place. She discovers a new bus stop and hopes it will take her to her friend, Madison. Instead, it stops at Greenlake. Nina sees a dog walker and asks, "Have you seen Madison?"

The dog walker says, "Oh, yes, I live there. Madison Park is quite lovely."

"Oh, no," says Nina, "my friend, Madison…he got on a different bus."

"Try that bus, dear," points the dog walker.

Nina tries yet another bus. She is feeling tired and hopes this bus is headed to Lake Forest Park and home. "I am ready for a nap," Nina yawns to herself.

"Me too," says a familiar voice.

"Madison? Madison!"

"Is that you, Nina? I am so happy to see you!"

After their adventure,
Nina and Madison understand

why it is important to hold hands
when getting on and off the bus.

Photo taken by Nora - age 7.

Tara Jorgensen is a Seattle native with a love for her city. She is a current resident of its local suburb, Lake Forest Park. Upon graduating from writing school, she completed this book.

Tara is a mother of two young children. Nora and Anders love to paint and draw. She has been inspired by them, as well as her students at Ms. Tara's Preschool to create *Nina and Madison.*

A portion of the proceeds from this book will be donated to Children's Hospital in Seattle, Washington.

Nina and MADISON

Ride the Bus in Seattle

by **Tara Jorgensen**

I.S.B.N. 1-59879-329-2

Order Online at:
www.authorstobelievein.com
www.amazon.com
www.barnesandnoble.com
or taralance@aol.com

By Phone Toll Free at:
1-877-843-1007

Special thanks to Lifevest Publishing,
Kat Spellman and the Spellman Company,
Megan Meno, and Jennifer King for Editing